Santa's HAT

by Linda Bleck

For my loved ones who have encouraged me to wear different hats in my lifetime, especially my parents Tom and Virginia

Printed in China

Books published by Running Press are available at special discounts for bulk purchases in the United States by corporations, institutions, and other organizations. For more information, please contact the Special Markets Department at the Perseus Books Group, 2300 Chestnut Street, Suite 200, Philadelphia, PA 19103, or call (800) 810-4145, ext. 5000, or e-mail special.markets@perseusbooks.com.

ISBN 978-0-7624-4292-8

Library of Congress Control Number: 2011941450

E-book ISBN 978-0-7624-4632-2

9 8 7 6 5 4 3 2 1
Digit on the right indicates the number of this printing

Cover and interior design by Ryan Hayes
Edited by Marlo Scrimizzi
Typography: Typography of Coop

Published by Running Press Kids
An Imprint of Running Press Book Publishers
A Member of the Perseus Books Group
2300 Chestnut Street
Philadelphia, PA 19103–4371

Visit us on the web!
www.runningpress.com

Santa's HAT

by Linda Bleck

RP|KIDS
PHILADELPHIA • LONDON

Today was Christmas Eve and the North Pole's annual snow festival. Everyone—from the elves to the snow bunnies to the reindeer—participated. Santa's favorite part was watching the snowman building event.

"Put a hat on if you're going outside," Mrs. Claus
said to Santa. "You don't want to catch another cold."

"I can't find my hat," said Santa.
"I've looked everywhere for it."

"Wear one of these," said Mrs. Claus, and she opened a chest full of hats. Santa's dogs, Bell and Bow, pawed through the hats of all different shapes and sizes.

"Hmm . . . ," thought Santa. "I guess
I could try a new hat for the day."

Santa began trying on each hat. . . .

One hat was too silly.

One hat was too wide.

Another was too scary.

That hat was too tight.

The other hat was too big.

This one was too fancy.

Then he pulled out a baseball cap. "This could be good for sliding in the snow," Santa said.

Next he found a hockey helmet.
"Watch me get a hat trick!"
he shouted to Bell and Bow.

When Santa donned a cowboy hat,
he exclaimed, "Oh silver spurs, maybe
this hat will do! Giddy up, Blitzen!"

Then Santa slipped on a detective's hat
and looked around the room.

"Let's find out who's naughty
or nice this year."

"All aboard!" Santa shouted, as he fit
a train conductor's hat on his head.
"Choo, choo, full steam ahead!"

"Here, Santa, how about this one?" Mrs. Claus slipped a cap on Santa that she had knitted for him that day.

"My favorite colors, and it will keep my ears warm," Santa said.

Santa ran outside to look at all the snowmen.

The elves were putting on the finishing touches. It looked just like Santa, and he was holding a present in his arms.

"What do you think?" asked the elves.

"I think something is missing," said Santa.

One of the elves
pointed to the box.

"A present for me?"
Santa said as he
opened it.

"Ho! Ho! Ho!" chuckled Santa.
"It's a perfect fit!"

And Bell and Bow agreed.

Later that night . . .

"Have you got your list, Santa?"